I SURVIVED

THE GALVESTON HURRICANE, 1900

by Lauren Tarshis

illustrated by Scott Dawson

Scholastic Inc.

For Katie Woehr

Text copyright © 2021 by Dreyfuss Tarshis Media Inc.

Illustrations copyright © 2021 by Scholastic Inc.

Photos ©: 118 top: Courtesy of the Rosenberg Library, Galveston, Texas; 118 bottom: Tim Leviston/EyeEm/Getty Images; 120: Courtesy of the Rosenberg Library, Galveston, Texas; 123: Library of Congress/Getty Images; 125: Archive Photos/Getty Images; 128: NASA/GSFC/Phil Degginger/Color-Pic/Alamy Stock Photo; 130: Oleksandr Tikki/Getty Images; 132: National Archives; 133, 134: Courtesy of the Rosenberg Library, Galveston, Texas; 137 top: Hi-Story/ Alamy Stock Photo; 137 bottom: Keith Corrigan/Alamy Stock Photo.

Special thanks to Jami Durham, Dale Carnegie, Casey Green, and Lauren Martino Henry.

This book is being published simultaneously in paperback by Scholastic Press.

ISBN 978-1-338-75254-0

10 9 8 7 6 5 4 3 2 1

21 22 23 24 25

Printed in the U.S.A.

113

First printing 2021

Designed by Katie Fitch

CHAPTER 1

SATURDAY, SEPTEMBER 8, 1900
AROUND 7:00 P.M.
GALVESTON, TEXAS

Noooooooooo!

A powerful blast of wind grabbed hold of eleven-year-old Charlie Miller and threw him into the raging flood. He screamed for his parents and his little sister as the churning waters swept him away.

Charlie was caught in the jaws of the deadliest natural disaster ever to hit the United States. A vicious hurricane was destroying the beautiful city of Galveston, Texas. Winds tore apart houses and buildings. Towering waves crashed over streets. Thousands of people were already dead. And now the screaming winds and drowning waters had come for Charlie.

Charlie sputtered and gasped as he struggled to keep his head above the waves. But the water was filled with wreckage. Every second something smacked him, scraped him, stabbed him. A chunk of roof. A wagon wheel. Hunks of wood and glass. All that was left of houses and shops he'd known all his life.

Charlie managed to grab hold of a floating door and climb on top. But now he faced the killer wind, which had turned bricks and tiles into cannonballs. Charlie flattened himself against the cold, wet wood, squeezing his eyes shut. Even the pouring rain couldn't wash away his tears.

Charlie had never felt so terrified, or alone.

Just that morning, none of this had seemed possible. Galveston was one of the most important cities in Texas. Nobody believed a big hurricane could strike here.

But then came the monstrous waves.

Ba-room!

The wind that blasted with shrieking gusts.

Whoo-eeeeesh! Whoo-eeeeesh! Who-eeeeesh!

The sky turned black and split apart. Rain gushed down. But most shocking was when the usually peaceful Gulf of Mexico suddenly rose up — higher, higher, higher — and swallowed the city.

Galveston was doomed.

Charlie looked frantically around him. Where were Mama and Papa and his little sister, Lulu? Were they somewhere out here, too?

Lightning flashed, each bolt lighting up a new horror floating by.

Flash!

A house on its side.

Flash!

A woman clinging to a pile of wood.

Flash!

A huge wooden pole, speeding through the water.

Heading right for Charlie.

CHAPTER 2

FOUR DAYS EARLIER
TUESDAY, SEPTEMBER 4, 1900
AROUND 2:00 P.M.
CHARLIE'S HOUSE
GALVESTON, TEXAS

It was a hot and sticky afternoon, and Charlie was alone in his room. His two-year-old sister, Lulu, was supposed to be napping. But she was singing away in her bed across the hall. *"La, la, la . . . La, la, la."*

Mama and Papa's sunny voices drifted from the kitchen.

Busy city sounds rose up from the streets — the *clop, clop, clop* of horses, the squeaks and rumbles of wagons, boys whooping as they played marbles in the alley.

But Charlie barely heard. He was busy practicing his magic.

One by one Charlie went through his tricks — the disappearing coin, the vanishing balls, the floating card. He'd been practicing all summer. His best friend, Sarah, said he should try out for the talent show at school. But there was no way Charlie would do that. That was something Sarah would do, not Charlie.

As for magic, he'd barely thought about it until a few months ago, when Mama and Papa took him to see a magician named Antonio Meraki. Charlie had heard of him, of course — he was practically as famous as President McKinley. And the moment Meraki stepped onto the stage, Charlie understood why.

Whoosh! Meraki threw a card into the air, and suddenly it was a yellow bird, fluttering around the theater.

Presto! He took a stick, waved his hands, and the stick magically turned into a tree covered with big white flowers.

He made a lady float up into the air, turn somersaults near the ceiling, and gently float back down.

But the best came near the end. Meraki asked a lady from the audience if he could borrow her ring. He put it into a pouch and smashed it with a hammer. He sprinkled the sparkling crumbs into the barrel of a gun.

Pow! Meraki shot the gun at a box hanging at the edge of the stage. He opened the box — and there was the ring, good as new.

The crowd went wild.

Charlie just sat there in shock.

That's impossible! he thought.

And of course he knew it was. None of those things had *really* happened. That's what a magic trick was — a trick. Behind each one was some secret — a special prop or cleverly built box, a hidden mirror or trapdoor, wires or ropes the audience couldn't see.

A magician made impossible things look . . . possible.

Charlie wanted to be a magician!

He bought himself a beginner's magic kit and Meraki's book, *The Secrets of Magic*.

He tried doing some basic tricks. But he stank! He could barely shuffle a deck of cards. Coins clattered noisily to the floor. The vanishing balls got stuck in their jars.

So Charlie put the kit away.

But then a few weeks later, he picked up Meraki's book. The magician's picture was on the cover — a bald man with a thick brown mustache and bright blue eyes. The book was long, but definitely not boring. It turned out that Meraki's life was as exciting as his show.

He was born on a farm with nothing, lived with his mean uncle, and ran away from home when he was ten. By fifteen, he was performing in circus shows. By twenty, he'd traveled the world. Since then, he'd survived cobra bites, storms at sea, and enemies willing to kill him to steal his tricks.

In his chapter about how to do magic, Meraki wrote:

The road to fame wasn't easy. I was a failure at magic at first. But I practiced. And that is the first secret that every young magician must learn: to practice.

Practice? Charlie had thought. Practice was for boring stuff, like the piano. He'd stunk at that, too — and quit.

But Meraki was right. Charlie practiced his magic tricks, and he got better. And there was something else. Doing his magic tricks gave Charlie a feeling — a bright and strong feeling — that he was more than just the shy boy afraid to talk to kids at school.

And speaking of school, it was starting in just two weeks. He hoped Sarah was in his class. But then Charlie thought of another kid at school — Gordon Potts. His stomach twisted. His cards slipped from his hand. Would Gordon start picking on Charlie again?

Charlie sat down on his bed and pictured Gordon — an overgrown goon with shadowy eyes and a puffed-up chest. Gordon was always making some poor chump's life miserable. And toward the end of last school year, that miserable chump was Charlie.

Gordon had started tormenting Charlie last spring, and it went on until the last day of school. Happily, Gordon had been gone all summer. His family was rich and had a mansion in the mountains somewhere. But what would happen when Gordon got back?

Charlie bent down to pick up his cards. If only magic were real. He'd make Gordon disappear. Or turn him into a frog — no, a fly. A fly on the rear end of a big sweaty horse.

Feeling better, Charlie took a breath and stood up. He shuffled the cards — they seemed to purr in his hands.

Charlie looked into the mirror. His familiar freckled face stared back at him. He imagined he was on a stage, lit up by glittering lights.

"Ladies and gentlemen," he said, in barely a whisper. "I am Charles the Great . . ."

Boom!

A clap of thunder exploded through the air.

Charlie put down his cards and ran to the open window. Sure enough, thick gray clouds swarmed the sky. Wind blasted Charlie's face. And here came the pouring rain. Charlie shut his window so the floor wouldn't get soaked.

Boom! Boom! More thunder shook the house.

And then, from across the hall, came the bone-chilling screams.

"Ahhhhhhhhhhhhh!"

CHAPTER 3

Charlie rushed to his little sister's room. He found Lulu under the bed, wailing in fear.

This was what Charlie hated about these storms — poor Lulu always got so scared!

Charlie never used to care about bad weather. Sure, it could be annoying when a storm suddenly swept in. Sometimes when it rained hard, the streets would flood. That's why almost all the houses and stores in Galveston were built up off the ground. Water would rush underneath, without wrecking what was inside. The wooden sidewalks were built up, too, two feet higher than the streets.

Storms were just a part of life here in Galveston. Charlie knew that. But lately the sight of gray clouds filled Charlie with dread. Because the slightest rumble of thunder sent his little sister into these fits of terror.

"Chowie!" she wailed from her hiding place.

That's what she called him. *Chowie.*

"The cloud monster!" she cried. "*Ahhhhhhhh!* The cloud monster!"

Lulu thought a bloodthirsty beast lived in the clouds and that every crack and boom of thunder was its ferocious roar.

Charlie gently slid Lulu out from under the bed. He scooped her up and held her. Mama and Papa came in. Mama put her hand on Lulu's sweaty head, and Papa patted her back.

"I'll take care of her," Charlie said to his parents.

"Are you sure?" Mama asked.

Charlie nodded — he usually managed to calm Lulu down.

Mama and Papa left, and Charlie tried singing Lulu a song.

"The itsy, bitsy spider . . ."

"Cloud monster!"

"Mary had a little lamb . . ."

"Cloud monster!"

Nothing was working.

Charlie thought of the magician Meraki. One of Charlie's favorite chapters in Meraki's book was when Meraki was on a big ship, heading back to America from India.

The ship sailed into a giant storm. Massive waves rose up and crashed over the ship's deck. The passengers huddled below, terrified. And what did Meraki do? He put on a magic show, of course, distracting the audience with his dazzling tricks.

Charlie's tricks weren't very dazzling. Then again, Lulu got all excited when she saw a ladybug.

"Lulu!" he said. "Can you help me find my magic coin?"

Sniff. "The cloud —"

"My magic coin, Lulu! I think you have it!"

Lulu loosened her iron grip. She wiped her runny nose on Charlie's shirt.

"Where the coin, Chowie?" she asked.

Charlie's idea was working! But it also could be that the storm was already losing strength. The booms had turned to low rumbles.

Charlie gently plopped Lulu down so she was sitting at the edge of the bed.

"Is my coin inside your mouth?" he asked, brushing away her tears. "Open up."

She opened her gummy mouth and sent a puff of milky breath up Charlie's nose.

"Could it be here?" he said, checking between her fat little toes.

"How about here?" he asked, peeking under her chin, then inside her slimy nose.

"Hmmmmm," Charlie said.

Lulu's eyes were getting brighter. She pressed her lips together. She was trying not to giggle.

"Check under your pillow. I bet it's there," Charlie said.

Lulu turned and lifted up her pillow.

Charlie quickly reached into his pocket for the coin he always carried with him. He pushed

it firmly into the flat part of his palm, locking it into place. He whipped his hand out of his pocket and put it up near Lulu's ear. Flicking his hand slightly, he made the coin drop into his finger-tips. This magic move was known as the French drop, and it was one of the first tricks a beginner magician learned.

"Ah-ha!" Charlie said, holding the coin out to Lulu.

Lulu's eyes widened and she broke into a grin.

"Do again!" she said. "Do again!"

Charlie felt like taking a bow.

Ten minutes later, Charlie walked into the kitchen.

"Where's Lulu?" Mama asked.

"Asleep," Charlie said.

"How'd you do that?" Papa said.

"Magic trick," Charlie said. He shrugged.

Mama came over and gave him a kiss on the cheek. "When you're a famous magician, I'll be first in line for your autograph."

"I'll be second," Papa said.

"And look," Mama said. "The sun is out. The storm's over."

Charlie peered out the window. The sky was bright blue.

He wasn't fooled, though. This was Galveston.

There would always be another storm.

CHAPTER 4

A few minutes later, there was a knock on the door. Charlie answered it and found his best friend, Sarah, standing on his porch in her red-and-white-striped bathing costume. She was carrying a beat-up metal washtub.

"Come on!" Sarah said, flashing her very large front teeth. "I heard there's an amazing overflow."

"I'm coming!" Charlie said.

An overflow was a special kind of Galveston flood. Not from pouring rain — from the Gulf. Galveston sat on a small island. When Charlie saw the island on a map, he always thought of the noodles Mama made for their soup — long, skinny, and very flat. Their noodle island was twenty-seven miles long and only a mile wide in places. It sat on the Gulf of Mexico, about two miles from the main part of Texas.

There was water all around them — the Gulf to the south and Galveston Bay to the north.

Sometimes during storms and high tides, water from the Gulf overflowed and filled the streets near the beach.

There was nothing better than an overflow, especially in the steamy summer.

In a flash, Charlie had changed into his bathing shorts and tank top. He quickly peeped in on Lulu — still fast asleep — and waved goodbye to Mama and Papa.

"Have fun!" Papa said. He'd loved playing in the overflows when he was a kid.

"Let's go this way," Sarah said, taking the lead as they headed out from Charlie's house. Sarah had strong opinions about everything. Like back in kindergarten, when she announced that she and Charlie would be best friends forever. She could be pushy. But that didn't bother Charlie. He didn't have to think too hard when he was around Sarah.

The street was busy — clogged with all kinds of wagons and carriages and buggies. But Charlie was used to it. Every street in Galveston was busy these days — it was the fastest-growing city in all of the south. Papa had told Charlie that. He was always bragging about how great Galveston was.

Last night at dinner, Papa had looked up from his stew and said, "You know what I just heard? There are more millionaires in Galveston than in almost any other small city in the world."

Mama had waved her hand over her faded apron.

"Oh, indeed," she said in a fake fancy voice. "We millionaires *love* Galveston!"

That cracked them all up.

But Charlie got why Papa was proud. Who wouldn't want to live in Galveston? It was a city that had everything — restaurants and stores and theaters. They had their port, with big ships coming from all over the world.

Texas

West Bay

N
W · E
S

Gulf o

And the beach, of course — miles and miles of the prettiest beach in Texas. That's what everyone said about the beach, which was on the Gulf side of the island. There were hotels and shops along the beach, and even big bathhouses where you could dry off after swimming, change, and buy a snack.

The biggest and best bathhouse was the Pagoda, which Charlie could see now, in the distance. It was built out over the water of the Gulf, maybe thirty feet from the beach. You walked on a long, skinny raised walkway to get to it.

Charlie liked to imagine it was a floating palace.

"We should have brought Lulu," Sarah said, snapping Charlie out of his thoughts.

"She's napping," Charlie said. "The storm scared her. She thinks there's a monster in the sky." Charlie shook his head as her wails echoed through his mind. "It's really sad."

"It makes perfect sense to me," Sarah said, blowing a hunk of her thick brown hair out of her eyes. "Lulu doesn't understand what a thunderstorm is. And if you didn't understand the weather, a thunderstorm would be pretty terrifying — all that noise, and the clouds, and the lightning . . ."

Sarah was right. As usual.

"Think about it," Sarah said — she started half her sentences with those three words — *think about it*. "A long time ago, even the smartest people thought gods and goddesses controlled everything, including the weather."

"Gods like Poseidon," Charlie said, remembering the book of Greek myths Grandpa used to read to him.

"Exactly," Sarah said.

Charlie's heart cracked a little as he thought of his grandfather, who'd died last year. He was a hero of the Texas Revolution — he was always telling stories about the battles he'd fought in. They all missed him.

Sarah grabbed Charlie's arm and let out a happy cry. "Look!"

The entire beach was covered with water, which had also crept up onto the streets. The water looked like it was three feet deep in places. It was like a gigantic swimming pool.

"Let's go!" Charlie shouted.

CHAPTER 5

AROUND 3:00
THE EDGE OF THE BEACH
GALVESTON, TEXAS

It seemed every kid in Galveston was in the water — swimming, splashing, floating on a raft or tub, racing a toy boat. Charlie and Sarah waded to the middle of the street, where the water came halfway up Charlie's thighs.

"This is the spot," Sarah announced, plopping the washtub down. She climbed inside and sat with her legs crossed. Charlie gave the tub a spin, and Sarah whirled around. Charlie floated around on his back while Sarah spun around in the tub.

After a few minutes, he stood up and looked out at the Gulf. It had probably been churned up during the storm. But it was already calming down. Most days, the water seemed like a big, rippling pond.

The tub had stopped spinning, and Sarah drifted toward Charlie. She sighed. "Don't you think it would be fun to have a *real* ocean?" she said.

"This is a real ocean," Charlie said. "The Gulf is part of the Atlantic Ocean."

"I know that," Sarah said, giving Charlie a look. "I meant with big waves we could ride on top of. Like in Hawaii."

They'd learned about Hawaii in school. It was a bunch of islands in the Pacific that had just become a territory of the United States. Their teacher had showed them a picture of someone in Hawaii riding on top of a giant wave on a long wooden board.

Sarah stood up in the tub and held out her arms, like the people in the picture.

"Look! I'm riding the waves!" she shouted. And then she teetered. "Whoooa!" She plopped into the water with a loud splash.

Charlie laughed.

He held out his hand and pulled her to her feet.

"Look," she said, giving Charlie a nudge. "There she is."

Charlie followed Sarah's gaze over to three girls from their class last year. His cheeks got hot when he recognized the one in the middle:

Rosemary Cline. Charlie had a crush on her, and Sarah knew it.

Rosemary had one of the best singing voices in their class. Plus, her dad was kind of famous; he was the chief of Galveston's weather office. He'd come to their class last year to give a talk on weather. It was pretty interesting. He talked about different storms. Sarah asked about the big hurricane that had recently hit Puerto Rico, a big island not so far from Florida.

They'd all heard about it, of course. Thousands of people were killed. Mama's church group collected clothes and money to send there.

"Hurricanes are the most powerful storms in nature," Mr. Cline had said. "But we never have to worry about a big hurricane hitting Galveston. It's impossible."

Everyone in Galveston knew this — Mr. Cline was always being quoted in the newspaper.

Charlie looked out at the Gulf now, remembering how Mr. Cline had explained it to them. He said that most big Atlantic Ocean hurricanes follow the same path. They form off the coast of

Africa, chug across the Atlantic, then sweep over Florida and the East Coast of the United States.

"These hurricanes can't reach Galveston, because the winds will always pull them north," he said. "And if a powerful storm does enter the Gulf, Galveston can't be damaged. This part of the Gulf is too shallow for there to be truly powerful waves."

Charlie looked at the puny little waves now. It would be fun to have huge waves to ride on. But it was better not to have to worry about hurricanes.

Sarah gave Charlie a little shove.

"Go say hi to Rosemary."

Charlie shook his head.

He liked Rosemary. But that didn't mean he actually wanted to *talk* to her!

Plus, the overflow was ending — the water starting to rush back into the Gulf. Soon the streets would be dry, and kids would be building sand castles on the beach.

The current tugged hard on Charlie's legs, like it wanted to take him for a ride.

He hopped into the tub. If he was lucky, he

could ride the current all the way from this flooded street, down the beach, and into the Gulf.

Sarah gave the tub a big heave. It lurched forward, and off Charlie went. *Zip!* Sarah ran alongside him as he went rushing across the flooded road and down the beach toward the Gulf. He closed his eyes, imagining he was riding a huge Hawaiian wave.

But before Charlie made it to the Gulf, Sarah screamed out.

"Charlie! Watch out!"

Charlie's eyes popped open. Was there a snake somewhere? That was one bad thing about overflows — underground creatures sometimes got washed into the streets or onto the beach.

Mostly they were harmless bullfrogs and garter snakes. But last year a kid playing in an overflow got bitten by a water moccasin. The kid was lucky because the snake was pretty small and his friends got him to the hospital quick.

Charlie looked up, and his blood turned cold. It was not a snake.

It was something much worse.

CHAPTER 6

Gordon Potts.

He was standing in Charlie's path. In his hands he gripped an enormous branch. The pointy tip was aimed right at Charlie's chest.

A hot streak of fear shot through Charlie as he threw himself to one side. The move tipped over the washtub, dumping Charlie into the water. With a sickening clang, one of the washtub handles smacked Charlie right in the mouth.

He gagged as blood and salt water rushed down his throat.

He came up coughing and sputtering. He

struggled to his feet, and Sarah took him by the arm. His eyes stung, and everything was a blur.

"Stop blubbering," Gordon taunted. "You're so weak!"

Then he broke out in his high, earsplitting cackle.

Haw! Haw! Haw!
Haw! Haw! Haw!

Was this really funny to him? Charlie bleeding and choking?

"Hey, Gordon, come on!" another kid shouted. And Gordon disappeared.

Sarah led Charlie away from the water and off the beach. The water was all gone, leaving behind a mucky soup. They headed back toward Charlie's house.

Charlie's whole mouth throbbed. To his amazement — and relief — all his teeth were still attached. His bottom lip felt nasty. It was split and swollen.

Sarah didn't say anything as they walked along the crowded sidewalk. And when she finally looked at Charlie, her eyes didn't have their usual gleam.

"Gordon could have —" Her voice cracked. "He could have really hurt you, Charlie."

Charlie pictured that huge, pointed stick. Sarah was right.

Just then, he noticed an old man in a worn green hat hobbling toward them on the sidewalk. It was Mr. Early, one of Grandpa's friends. Charlie ducked his head down; he didn't want Mr. Early to see him this way.

Out of the corner of his eye, Charlie saw Mr. Early look right at him. But somehow the old man didn't recognize him. Probably because Charlie's face was so battered and bloody. He must look like he'd been kicked by a horse.

A lump grew in Charlie's throat, but he managed to fight back his tears. Why did Gordon pick on *him*?

He'd never done anything to Gordon — or to anyone! He wasn't a show-off or a teacher's pet. He never chased girls around the playground or tried to push his way into marbles games. Charlie was just . . . Charlie. Except for Sarah, nobody even really noticed him. It was true that he sometimes wished they did, that he got invited to birthday parties, that girls like Rosemary Cline would choose him as a square-dance partner.

But he was fine keeping mostly to himself.

What did he do to make Gordon suddenly hate him so much?

Over and over, Charlie had searched his mind for reasons. And he always came back to one night last May. Charlie had been out for an after-supper walk with Mama, Papa, and Lulu.

Mama and Lulu were softly singing a song, and Papa and Charlie were laughing over some dumb joke they'd shared. In fact, they were laughing so hard people they passed were shooting them strange looks. This happened all the time.

"Can you two please have a little less fun?" Mama had said. But she was smiling, too.

As they were passing an expensive restaurant, a fancy-looking man and a woman came out onto the sidewalk. A boy was trailing behind them, and the man was scolding him.

"I won't tolerate this!"

Charlie realized it was Mr. and Mrs. Potts — and

Gordon. Charlie wasn't surprised that Gordon was in trouble with his father. Gordon was rude to everyone — even their teacher. And people said Mr. Potts was pretty nasty himself. Papa had done some carpentry work in his office. "That guy screams at everyone!" he'd said.

But Mrs. Potts was sweet. She and Mama had become friends when they worked together at church to collect clothes to send to Puerto Rico. Mama had even gone to the Pottses' house for lunch. They lived in one of the big mansions lined up along Broadway.

"They have electricity in every room," she'd told Charlie and Papa later.

At Charlie's house, they still used kerosene lanterns.

"They have a telephone, too!"

Charlie's family didn't have one of those either. Papa said those were just silly toys, a waste of money.

"They'll never catch on," he'd said.

But Mama had kept the best part for last. "They have a toilet . . . that flushes!"

Even Papa was impressed with that. Charlie's family still used their privy, a little shack a few feet outside the back door of their house. Inside was a hole in the ground, with a wooden seat on top.

It wasn't too bad, except for hot days in the summer. And the time Charlie opened the door and there were two raccoons inside.

On that night outside the restaurant, Mrs. Potts had smiled and waved, and Mr. Potts had said a gruff hello.

"I hope you'll come over again soon!" Mrs. Potts had called to Mama. "Please drop by anytime. I'm still dreaming about those gingersnaps you brought!"

Charlie had noticed that Gordon ignored them all. But that wasn't unusual. Gordon had never paid any attention to Charlie.

Until the very next day, when it all started. Gordon glared at Charlie. Shoved him on the way out of recess. Pelted him with spitballs. Each day was a little worse.

Sarah convinced Charlie to tell their teacher. The day after that, Gordon called to Charlie.

"Hey! I have a friend for you!"

Charlie looked over.

Thud. Something hit him in the stomach — a dead rat. A big, rotting rodent crawling with maggots.

Luckily school ended the next day, and Gordon disappeared from Galveston.

Charlie shivered now as he and Sarah walked along, even though the sun was blasting down. Sarah looped her arm through Charlie's.

Charlie had hoped Gordon would forget about him over the summer.

Obviously he was wrong.

CHAPTER 7

LATER THAT NIGHT
AROUND MIDNIGHT

Charlie opened his eyes and heard Lulu screaming.

"The cloud monster! The cloud monster!"

He looked out the window, and a hideous green cloud was swirling in the sky. All of a sudden, it twisted into a giant face. A giant, sneering face . . . a face Charlie recognized.

"Aaaaaaaahhhh!" Charlie screamed.

And then everything went dark. Charlie's

heart pounded. Where was Lulu? Why was it suddenly so quiet? And wait. Where *was* he?

In bed, he realized. He'd had a nightmare. Charlie put his hand on his chest and took a deep breath.

This is bad, he thought.

Gordon had tormented him at school. At the beach . . . and now in his dreams!

Charlie got out of bed and took deep breaths. He glanced in the mirror above his dresser. Even in the dim light of the moon, Charlie could see his swollen lip in the reflection. He didn't look like Charles the Great. He looked like Charles the Ugly.

Charles the Scared.

Charles the Weak.

A few tears slipped out. He wiped them away. *Enough*, he told himself.

He sat down on his bed, switched on his lantern, and reached for Meraki's book.

Reading about Meraki's life always made him feel better. He'd had a rough time, too, and look at him! The most famous magician in the world.

One of the best chapters was near the end, when Meraki was kidnapped by two men. Charlie settled back on his pillow and started to read.

I was walking home from a show, enjoying the night, and two men stopped me. They both had guns, and they ordered me to walk with them to a filthy building. I figured out very quickly that they did not want my money. They had been sent by my enemy. He's a magician named Thedo the Powerful. For years he'd been trying to steal the secret of my most popular trick: The Floating Woman. It had taken me years to create that trick. It was my treasure.

Thedo had sent spies to my shows in the past. They'd broken into my hotel rooms looking for the sketches of how the trick was done. And now he'd sent these brutes.

The men took me to a small room, sat me down at a table, and shoved a notebook in front of me.

"Write it down," the taller of the men demanded.

"A magician never reveals his secrets!" I replied.

"Tell us or we'll shoot you," the other man said.

I almost gave up. I picked up the pencil and began to

draw the trick. But then a voice whispered through my mind — my own voice.

You have power.

But what power could that be? I wondered. These men were very strong. They both had guns. And then it came to me: my magic skills.

I could use magic to trick them. To scare them into letting me go. I thought hard, and somehow came up with a plan.

Luckily I always carried a few small props with me — cards, some coins, and a small vial of red liquid called magic blood. The vial was made of the thinnest glass. It was meant to be easily broken during a trick, and the shards would disappear into dust.

I stood up. "I was raised by a family of snake charmers," I said to the men. (This was not true, of course, but the men didn't know that.)

"I was bitten by cobras many times," I continued. (In fact I had been bitten only once by a cobra, while visiting a village in India.)

"The venom gave me powers," I told the men. (Quite the opposite, that cobra bite had nearly killed me.)

"And now, if you do not let me go, I will use my cobra powers to take all of the blood from your bodies. Every drop."

I used a low, rasping voice. I flicked my tongue several times in a snakelike way. I swayed my body slightly, as a cobra does when it rises from a snake charmer's basket. I rolled my eyes up into my head so that only the whites showed.

The men looked at each other in confusion. And here was my chance. I snuck my hand into my pocket and grabbed

the fake blood. Keeping it hidden in my hand, I reached up to the taller man's head, right next to his ear. I squeezed the vial so it cracked. The magic blood sprayed onto the man's face, the wall, and the ceiling. It was a gruesome show.

The men ran screaming from the room. I rushed to the police.

Thedo never bothered me again.

My floating woman trick was safe.

Charlie slowly closed the book. His whole body tingled.

You have power. It was like Meraki's voice was whispering inside his head.

And that's when it came to Charlie — he could trick Gordon like Meraki had tricked his kidnappers.

Charlie lay there for hours thinking, turning ideas over and over in his mind.

By morning, he had his plan. He'd need a few days to prepare.

But soon, everything was going to change.

CHAPTER 8

```
FOUR DAYS LATER
SATURDAY, SEPTEMBER 8, 1900
AROUND 9:30 A.M.
CHARLIE'S HOUSE
```

"Doing anything exciting today?" Papa asked Charlie, peering up over the newspaper.

Lulu was stuffing a pancake into her mouth, and Mama was sipping her coffee. They all looked at Charlie.

"I'm going to the Pagoda," Charlie said, which

wasn't a lie. That's where he'd find Gordon on a Saturday morning, for sure. Of course, Mama and Papa had no idea what Charlie *actually* planned to do today.

Neither did Sarah. She definitely wouldn't approve of his plan. Luckily she and her family had gone to Houston for the weekend. Sarah was now fifty miles away.

"Thank goodness it's cooler today," Mama said, sliding another pancake onto Lulu's plate. Yesterday had been brutal, one of the hottest days of the summer.

Papa nodded. "Seems like the temperature dropped ten degrees before the sun came up."

"Speaking of sunrise," Mama said, eyeing Charlie. "What got you out of bed so early?"

Charlie gulped. He had been up early, but he hadn't thought Mama or Papa had heard him.

"Um, I . . ." *Think fast.* "I just needed a drink of water. Then I went back to sleep."

He couldn't tell them the real reason: He'd crept into the kitchen to get some cockroaches. Dead ones. He needed them for the trick that was going to terrify Gordon Potts into leaving him alone.

Finding cockroaches in Galveston was never a problem — they were everywhere, even in Mama's spotless kitchen. Charlie quickly found three dead ones under the stove. He had them in his pocket now, tucked inside a box.

Papa put his newspaper down on the table. "Well, it's a good thing we're not in Florida. Says here in the weather report there's a very bad storm there."

"A storm?" Lulu said, her eyes suddenly wide.

"No, darling," Mama said, shooting Papa her *don't scare Lulu* look.

"Not anywhere near here," Papa said, giving Lulu's cheek a gentle pat. "We might just get a little rain."

Charlie leaned over and read the weather report for Galveston.

Rain Saturday and Sunday. Some winds from the north.

Papa was telling Lulu the truth. No storms today. Which was a relief. Because a storm would keep Gordon away from the Pagoda — and ruin Charlie's plan.

An hour later, Charlie was on his way to the beach. Eyeing the cloudy sky, Charlie decided it definitely looked like rain. But anything was better than yesterday's sticky heat.

As usual, the street was packed. But Charlie barely noticed. In his mind, he was going through his trick. He'd spent hours working it out, practicing over and over in the mirror. He felt like Meraki, rehearsing for a big show.

He'd stalk Gordon, stride up to him, and stare right into his eyes.

"Gordon Potts," he'd say, in a low, steady voice. "Did you know it's possible to put a cockroach into a person's skull? It's an ancient trick I've mastered."

Then he would pull the cockroach from his pocket, wave it in front of Gordon's eyes, and whip it right up next to Gordon's ear. He'd make sure Gordon felt the creature's spindly legs and antennae on his ear.

But then Charlie would secretly let the

cockroach slip back into his palm, a French drop. Gordon would think the cockroach had vanished — *into his skull.*

Gordon would be good and spooked, and Charlie would finish off the trick.

"I will remove the cockroach from your brain," he'd say. "If you vow never to bother me again. I'll give you five seconds to decide — before the cockroach can lay its eggs."

That egg-laying part — Charlie was especially proud of that touch.

If — when — Gordon swore to leave Charlie alone, Charlie would reach up to Gordon's ear and pretend to pluck something out. Finally, he would reveal the cockroach that had supposedly been inside Gordon's skull.

Charlie smiled to himself now as he made his way along the crowded sidewalk. He wasn't even that scared. Still, his heart was really thumping. His whole body seemed to be vibrating. His ears echoed with a low, pounding boom.

Ba-ROOM, ba-ROOM, ba-ROOM.

But it wasn't his heart.

Charlie realized this as soon as the beach came into view. He stared ahead, his eyes wide. That sound . . . it was coming from the Gulf of Mexico. Even from ten blocks away, he could see them.

Waves. Giant waves. Bigger even than in the pictures of Hawaii.

He blinked hard, wondering if his eyes were playing tricks. Was this some kind of mirage?

But no. They were waves, towering up, foaming, crashing down.

Ba-ROOM.

Ba-ROOM.

Ba-ROOM.

He stared in amazement, almost hypnotized. He'd been born in Galveston. He'd spent half his life on this beach. He'd been through dozens of storms.

Bu he'd never seen anything like this.

CHAPTER 9

AROUND 10:15 A.M.
THE BEACH IN FRONT OF THE
PAGODA BATHHOUSE

There was a big overflow, even bigger than the one
that he and Sarah had played in a few days ago.
People were lined up on the sidewalk on the edge of
the water. Excited voices rose up over the thunder-
ing roar of the waves.

"Look at those huge rollers!" a man shouted,
pointing at the waves.

"Incredible!" cried a woman.

50

"Mama!" a little boy squealed. "Take me closer!"

Each wave towered up — as tall as Charlie's house — and then crashed down.

Ba-ROOM!

Ba-ROOM!

Ba-ROOM!

Kids weren't splashing and floating in the street like last time. Today's big game was to stand on the flooded beach, wait for the waves to rise up, and sprint away before a wave could crash down over you. Lots of kids were doing this, shrieking and laughing as they ran back and forth. A few bigger kids were at least halfway down the beach.

It looked fun — but Charlie had to admit that the waves scared him a little. The entire Gulf looked different — churning, foaming, furious.

He thought of Lulu's cloud monster. And what Sarah had said about how people once blamed storms on angry gods and goddesses.

Watching the crashing sea, it was easy for Charlie to imagine Poseidon standing above on a cloud, his long beard whipping in the wind, raising his arms to create each wave.

Ba-ROOM!

Ba-ROOM!

Ba-ROOM!

Charlie's stomach did a flip. Poseidon seemed *very* angry.

But no one else seemed worried. The whoops and claps of the excited crowd got louder with each enormous wave.

Charlie felt almost hypnotized by the waves — until he spotted a tall, beefy kid in the middle of the beach, one of the risk-takers closer to the Gulf. Even from the back, Charlie could tell his chest was puffed out.

Gordon.

Before he could lose his nerve, Charlie reached into his pocket. He plucked a cockroach from the box. He tucked the insect into his palm, locking it into place like he'd practiced. His hand was shaking — bad.

He waited for a lull between the waves — the big ones came every two minutes or so — then he took his chance. His knees wobbled as he waded onto the beach, where the water came up to his thighs.

The wind pushed against his back like an invisible hand.

Go. Go. Go.

Before he knew it, he was standing behind Gordon Potts. He took a breath and tapped Gordon on the shoulder. Gordon looked at Charlie with surprise, and then his usual sneer.

"What do you want, twerp?" He practically spat the question.

Charlie opened his mouth. But the words he'd practiced were all gummed up on his tongue.

"Did you know . . . ?" His voice was high and squeaky. "An ancient trick . . . cockroaches . . ."

Charlie's hand was suddenly slick with sweat. The cockroach slipped out and plopped into the water.

He looked up at Gordon, who seemed ready to pounce.

What had Charlie been thinking? He needed to get out of here. Now!

Some kids around them had the same idea. Most were laughing, but a few were shouting.

"Look out!"

"It's a big one!"

And then the sky seemed to disappear above Charlie as a giant wave towered up, bigger than any that had come before. It rose higher, higher, higher . . .

Charlie and Gordon turned to run. But this wave was too fast and too big. Charlie barely had enough time to take a breath before the wall of water curled over and swallowed him up.

CHAPTER 10

The churning, gritty water was everywhere at once — over Charlie, under Charlie, up his nose, down his throat. The salt water stung his cut lip.

Luckily the twisting ride didn't last long. The wave spat him off the beach. He rolled. He stopped just before he smacked into the edge of the raised sidewalk. He pulled himself up, amazed he wasn't hurt. He'd torn the knee of his trousers, but that was it.

Three younger kids had also been swept here by the wave.

"Let's do that again!" screamed the littlest one,

and they all took off back toward the beach.

Charlie glanced nervously around — scanning for Gordon. But he didn't spot him. Hopefully the wave had carried him all the way to Hawaii.

But no. Gordon had to be somewhere close. A sickening feeling swirled in his stomach. He had to get out of here before Gordon found him.

But first he had to catch his breath. Charlie climbed up onto the sidewalk and stood behind three young men. All around him, people were still cheering as the waves crashed down. These men screamed and clapped at each wave like they were at a baseball game.

But then an angry shout interrupted them.

"What are you laughing at?"

Charlie turned as an old man in a green hat hobbled toward them. Charlie was surprised to see it was Mr. Early, Grandpa's friend. He didn't seem to notice Charlie.

"This is a hurricane!" he scolded the men.

The word — *hurricane*. It jarred Charlie, as if Mr. Early had cursed.

The four men eyed one another.

"Don't worry, sir," said the loudest of the group. "Hurricanes can't hit us here in Galveston." He was talking to Mr. Early as if the old man were a toddler like Lulu.

"That's dead wrong!" Mr. Early growled. He frowned, as if he'd argued about this before. "A hurricane nearly destroyed the whole island in 1837. That was before Galveston was even a city. But I was here back then. I was right here, and I remember it."

He looked off into the distance.

"The wind tore houses apart. Water was everywhere, even where it had never gone before. And then the sea suddenly rose up, swallowed the entire island. So many lost . . ."

Mr. Early's voice trailed off. A strong gust of wind lifted his hat off his head, but the old man didn't notice. He seemed like he was far away from here in his mind. Charlie reached up and snatched the hat from the air before it blew away.

The men eyed Mr. Early impatiently — he'd

interrupted their fun. The loud man signaled to his two buddies, and they moved farther down the sidewalk.

Mr. Early didn't notice that, either.

"That tree — that's how I got through. I climbed up. Somehow I managed to hang on until the sun came up. And when the storm was done, there was nothing left. Nothing at all."

He stood there, staring at the waves, his thin white hair blowing in the wind.

Charlie waited until he was sure Mr. Early was done with his story.

"Mr. Early," Charlie said finally, speaking up over the gusts. "Here's your hat."

Mr. Early looked surprised. He took his hat, put it on, and smiled at Charlie.

"Do I know you, son?"

Charlie didn't know what to say. Of course Charlie knew him. Charlie had joined him and Grandpa on a few fishing trips. But then Charlie understood — Mr. Early's memory must be slipping away from him. The same had happened to Grandpa before he passed away.

I should help him get home, Charlie thought. But then Mr. Early tipped his hat and hobbled away. And before Charlie could go after him, a chorus of gasps rose up from the crowd.

"The Pagoda!" a woman shouted.

Charlie whipped around and stared out at the Pagoda . . . or what was left of it. Waves were attacking the building, clawing it, ripping it to pieces. The roof cracked apart. The long walkway twisted and split in two.

Charlie remembered once seeing a pack of dogs fighting over the body of a squirrel. The terrible snarls and growls. The swiping claws and bared teeth. The hunks of fur that flew through the air.

That's what the ocean looked like now — a pack of wild beasts, devouring a carcass. Soon nothing would be left of the Pagoda but its scattered bones.

A chill slowly rose through Charlie's body.

Mr. Early's story . . . could it be true?

The cheering had stopped, and it had started to rain.

The wind gusted even harder.

Whoosh!

A wave crashed.

Ba-ROOM.

Mr. Cline said that it was impossible for a hurricane to hit Galveston. But Mr. Early said he'd lived through one. Charlie suddenly didn't know what to think.

He turned and ran.

He had to get home, now.

CHAPTER 11

AROUND NOON

Charlie tried to walk fast, but the wind was getting stronger, and it was pushing hard against him. He shouldered his way forward, his head down. It had started to pour.

But as he made his way farther from the beach, he noticed that everything seemed . . . normal. Carriages and buggies rattled by like always. Kids stomped through puddles. The streetcar's jolly *ding, ding, ding* echoed from nearby.

And back home it seemed like just a

typical rainy Saturday. He found his family in the kitchen. Mama was baking her famous ginger-snaps. Papa was sitting at the table, organizing his tools. He was getting ready to start a big new building job on Monday.

Lulu was sitting next to Papa, her face sticky from the cookie-dough-covered spoon she was licking.

"Chowie!" Lulu sang to him when he walked into the kitchen.

Mama took one look at him and gasped. "Goodness! You're soaked!" she exclaimed, rushing out quickly and returning with a blanket.

"The Pagoda is gone," Charlie said as Mama wrapped the blanket around his shoulders.

"Gone?" Mama gasped. "What do you mean?"

"The waves at the beach are . . . huge. I've never seen the Gulf so rough," Charlie said. "They tore it apart."

He thought of those wild dogs again.

"How terrible!" Mama said.

Papa let out a long whistle and shook his head. He didn't look shocked, though.

"Every few years a big storm comes along," he said. "Some buildings get damaged. A few might get swept away. It's the price we pay for living on this beautiful island. They'll rebuild right away. They'll make the Pagoda even stronger. You'll see."

Charlie still felt uneasy.

"Could this be . . . a hurricane?" Charlie asked.

"Of course not," Papa said.

"What that?" Lulu asked, eyes wide with curiosity.

Mama raised her eyebrows with alarm, signaling to Papa and Charlie to stop the discussion — now. Of course she was right, Charlie knew. *Hurricane* was not a word any two-year-old needed to learn. *Especially* Lulu.

Mama wiped Lulu's hands and face and took her off for a nap.

Charlie started to follow them. He felt silly. And he needed to change his clothes.

But Papa waved for him to come back. He put down his screwdriver and pushed aside his big toolbox as Charlie sat next to him. He was cold, but being closer to Papa warmed him up.

"You all right, son?"

No, Charlie wanted to say. And he realized it wasn't only those giant waves and the torn-apart Pagoda that was making him feel sick. It was Gordon. But he couldn't tell Papa that.

"Big storms can be fierce," Papa said, taking hold of Charlie's hand. "I've told you all about the big storm we had in 1886."

Charlie nodded — Papa told that story as often as Grandpa talked about the Texas Revolution. It was a huge storm. Streets all along the beach flooded. The bay flooded, too. There was so much water downtown that ships were sailing in the streets.

"What I've never admitted to you, or anyone, is that I was completely terrified," Papa said.

He peeked out the doorway, like he wanted to make sure Mama wasn't listening.

"I was maybe seventeen years old. A big show-off. Nothing scared me!" He smiled a little and then shook his head. "But the sound of that wind, and all that water. I was so scared I got into bed and huddled under the covers."

64

He chuckled softly.

"I was just like Lulu. I'm surprised I didn't hide under the bed."

Charlie cracked a smile, even though he could tell Papa wasn't kidding.

"I somehow managed to fall asleep," Papa went on. "And when I woke up? The sun was shining. We'd lost some tree branches. There was a mess in the yard. But we cleaned it all up."

The wind let out a big blast, and the window rattled.

Papa looked at it and waved his hand like he was shooing a fly. "This will be over soon. Don't worry."

Charlie took a breath. The air smelled like gingersnaps.

"Now, hurry up and change out of those wet clothes," Papa said. "Or Mama's going to make you wipe all the water off the kitchen floor."

Charlie felt much better. He changed, ignoring the sounds of the pounding rain and howling wind. Luckily there was no thunder. He peeked in on Lulu — she'd fallen right to sleep.

He figured he'd help Papa with his tools, but first he needed to use the privy. Never fun in weather like this. He opened the back door. The fierce wind sent a stinging spray of rain right into his eyes. He blinked hard as he took four steps to the privy and grabbed hold of the door handle.

The wooden handle felt slimy and lumpy. He figured it was clumps of mud. But then the lumps started to squirm under his fingers . . . they were alive!

Charlie jumped back in horror. Something shot toward him and slapped him on the cheek. It made a noise, a croaking hiss.

"Ahhhhh!" Charlie cried out.

He looked around, and now he could see that there were brown lumps everywhere. On every rock, tree stump, and stick. He looked down. There was one on his boot!

It had big, bulging eyes.

CHAPTER 12

Charlie's shouts brought Mama and Papa out the back door.

Charlie stood there, pointing. "They're . . . fffffrogs!"

Small brown frogs. The kind they always saw in the grass or the fishing creeks or the street gutters after an overflow. There was nothing weird about seeing frogs — even three or four at once. But there were hundreds here!

"Goodness!" Mama said.

"Look at that!" Papa said. "I'm sure they're

just trying to get off the wet ground. This rain is *really* coming down."

Papa wasn't worried, and even Mama just shook her head.

"Go quickly and come right back," she said to Charlie.

Charlie went into the privy and tried not to think about how many frogs might be watching him. He did his business — quick — and hurried inside. He went into his room and closed the door. He had to change again.

Could this day get any weirder? He just

wanted this storm to end. He decided to take Papa's advice and get into bed. He lay there a long time — it seemed like hours. But he couldn't fall asleep. So finally he cracked open his Meraki book. He turned to a random page and started reading about a young magician Meraki had met in New York City. His name was Harry Houdini.

He calls himself an escape artist, and he has a remarkable act. He can free himself from any rope or chain, no matter how tightly it is knotted. I am certain he uses no blade or any tool. He wouldn't tell his secret. But he did say one must not panic or struggle when trying to get free from a rope. That will only make a knot tighter.

Whoooooosh!

Wow! *That* was a big gust. The whole house shook. Charlie put the book down. Even Meraki couldn't distract him from this storm. And it made him nervous lying here alone.

He found Mama and Papa in the sitting room. Mama was mending Charlie's torn trousers. Papa was now sorting through his box of nails. It was barely three o'clock, but it was so dark outside they'd lit the lanterns.

"Gingersnaps are done," Mama said, pointing to a small plate on the coffee table. "Help yourself."

Charlie felt too queasy to eat one.

He went to the front window and peered out. Through the thick curtain of rain, he saw the dark steel-gray clouds tumbling around in the sky. They hung so low Charlie felt like he could reach up and grab one.

Whoooooooosh!

The house shook, even harder than before. But Mama and Papa didn't even look up from their work.

Charlie peered out into the street. To his surprise, he saw rushing water. Had he ever seen so much water in the street in front of their house? Not that he could remember.

"Papa," he said. "There's *a lot* of water in the street."

Papa glanced up from his nails. "Makes sense, son," he said. "I haven't seen it rain this hard in years. I'll bet there are some pretty big puddles out there."

Charlie looked harder at the street. The water didn't look like a bunch of puddles. It looked like . . . a river.

He imagined that Sarah was right next to him. He heard her voice in his head.

Think about it . . . where could that water be coming from?

Before Charlie even knew what he was doing, he had rushed out the front door.

"What are you —" Mama called as the door closed behind him.

There were more little brown frogs out here, all over the front porch. They seemed to stare at Charlie as he carefully made his way down the porch steps, trying not to slip. He pushed against the wind and stepped onto the street.

He was shocked to find himself in water halfway up his thighs. It was rushing so fast Charlie almost fell over.

This definitely was *not* a puddle.

The wind and rain raked at Charlie's face. His

heart pounded. *What is happening?* And then he had an idea, something Sarah would definitely do.

He dipped his finger in the water, stuck it in his mouth.

His finger tasted salty. Just like he'd guessed — and feared — it would.

Now Charlie was sure. This water wasn't coming from the sky. It was coming from the Gulf.

But how was that possible? The Gulf was nearly *a mile* from here. As Charlie looked around him, he remembered what Mr. Early had said. The wind howled, but Charlie could still hear the old man's words in his mind.

"Water was everywhere, even where it had never gone before."

CHAPTER 13

"Charlie!" Papa bellowed from the porch. "Come in!"

Charlie rushed back up the steps, and Papa pulled him inside, closing the door tight.

"It's salt water!" Charlie said breathlessly as water streamed down his face. Mama grabbed the blanket again and wrapped it around Charlie's shoulders.

"It's coming from the Gulf!" Charlie went on. "It's an overflow. An overflow reached all the way here!"

Papa put his hand on Charlie's shoulder. "That's not possible," he said.

"Papa! I'm telling you!" Charlie said. "I tasted the water! It's salty!"

"Maybe the wind has carried some sea spray . . ." Papa said.

Charlie stepped forward,

"I saw Mr. Early this morning. He said that a bad hurricane hit here in 1837, before Galveston was even a city. What if that's happening again?"

Papa was actually starting to look annoyed, which was rare.

"Charlie," he said, clearly trying to keep his voice low. "Remember what Mr. Cline says about hurricanes. He's an expert. And Mr. Early . . ."

"Mr. Early has become very confused, sweetheart," Mama said gently.

"So was Grandpa!" Charlie said. "But he never made anything up!"

Charlie just realized this now. He explained it to Mama and Papa — how, yes, Grandpa was very confused in the months before he died. He didn't know where he was, or who was who.

"But he remembered all the important things that happened to him," Charlie said, "especially memories from when he was a little boy. And all those stories about the Revolution."

Just a week before he died, Grandpa had told Charlie his favorite story — from when he'd fought in the famous battle of San Jacinto. That was the battle that won the Revolution. It made Texas its own country for a few years until it became an American state in 1845.

"He told me that story a million times . . ." Charlie remembered how Grandpa had described cannonballs and bullets flying through the air. "He always told it the exact same way — even that last time. Not one detail was missing!"

Charlie paused. Mama and Papa were just staring at him. How could Charlie make them understand? Because with each passing second, Charlie felt more and more certain.

"This *is* a hurricane!" he cried.

And as if the wind agreed with Charlie, a powerful gust shook the house. The walls trembled. And then . . .

PLOOF.

A big chunk of plaster fell from the sitting room ceiling and landed in a powdery clump on the floor.

Papa ran over and stared at it. He looked from the plaster to Charlie to the window. Then back at the plaster again.

The next thing Charlie knew, Papa was out the front door.

"William!" Mama called after him, but Papa rushed down the porch steps. Mama and Charlie watched from the doorway as Papa waded into the street — like Charlie had. He tasted the water — like Charlie had.

He came back inside. Water streamed from his beard. Charlie took off his blanket and put it around Papa.

It was very quiet for a moment — even the wind seemed to be holding its breath. And then Papa looked at Charlie.

"This *is* different from 1886 — from any storm I've seen," he said. "That water in the streets — it's not from the rain. It's from the Gulf. You're right, son. This could very well be a hurricane. I'm sorry I didn't believe you before."

Charlie felt a strange mix of feelings. Relieved that Papa believed him. But also scared.

Papa eyed the broken plaster from the ceiling again. "This house wasn't built for a hurricane," he said. "I know because I helped Grandpa build it."

He took a breath. "We need to leave right away."

Mama nodded. "I'll get Lulu and pack some clothes."

"Where will we go?" Charlie asked.

Mama and Papa looked at each other, and Charlie could see they didn't have an answer.

Then Mama glanced at the plate of gingersnaps on the coffee table.

"I have an idea," she said.

Fifteen minutes later, they were making their way along Avenue M, heading toward one of the biggest and sturdiest houses in Galveston. Normally the walk would take maybe fifteen minutes. But the weather was getting worse by the minute. It was dark and cold. The wind was fierce. The rain poured down.

Water filled the streets and sloshed onto the sidewalks. They had to zigzag around fallen wires and branches that blocked their way. Mama had wrapped Lulu in blankets and held her tight against her chest. Papa hovered over all of them, watching out for the bricks and roof tiles that were falling from buildings and blowing from rooftops.

Finally, they made it to the mansion on Broadway. It was built on top of thick stone pillars that lifted the house at least six feet off the ground.

Compared to their little house, this was a fortress. Mama and Papa were sure they'd be safe here. But as Papa knocked on the door, Charlie worried about what would be waiting for him inside.

Because this wasn't just any big house.

It was Gordon Potts's house.

CHAPTER 14

Mrs. Potts welcomed them, and it was clear she would have invited them in even if Mama hadn't brought her a tin of gingersnaps. She smiled at Mama and grabbed her hand.

"I'm so happy you're here," she said. "We've opened the house to anyone who needs a safe place."

She brushed some rain from Lulu's curls and

waved for them to follow her. "Let's find you a place to change."

Mrs. Potts took them upstairs to a room so they could change into the dry clothes Mama had packed. (Charlie had lost track of how many times he'd changed today.)

On the way back downstairs, Papa couldn't resist peeping into the bathroom. They all stared at the toilet before moving on.

There were at least thirty people in the living room. But there was still plenty of space. The room was bigger than Charlie's entire five-room house. Lulu gaped at the fancy couches and chairs, the paintings on the wall, the vases filled with flowers.

"Is this a castle?" she asked.

"Yes," Charlie said.

And he meant it.

There were electric lamps all around the room, but they weren't lit up; Charlie guessed that the electricity was out all over the city. Lanterns gave the room just enough light so that Charlie could see the faces of the people around him.

He recognized most of them — families of kids who went to Charlie's school, people from church. There was Mr. Lutz, their butcher, and his family. There was Mrs. Butler, the teacher Charlie had been hoping to get this year. Women rocked babies. Men stood at the windows.

Charlie spotted Mr. Potts, lurking in the doorway of the living room.

"He doesn't look happy," Papa said. That was for sure. Mr. Potts scanned the room suspiciously, like he was sure someone was about to pocket one of the silver cups that lined the shelves.

Mama shook her head. "I don't know how Mrs. Potts lives with him. He is quite . . . unpleasant."

So is his son, Charlie thought.

As for Gordon, Charlie didn't see him anywhere. Probably he'd locked himself in his fancy bedroom and was eating his supper off a golden platter. Charlie hoped he'd stay there.

"The storm is getting stronger," Papa said softly.

Charlie had been thinking the same.

The rain was banging harder against the roof, as though hundreds of carpenters were up there, all pounding hammers at once.

The wind had taken on a new sound, a kind of roaring shriek.

Whoooooo-eeeeeesh!

"What that noise?" Lulu said, her eyes widening.

Uh-oh.

Up until now, Lulu had been amazingly calm.

It really was just thunder that scared her, and so far there hadn't been a single boom.

But with each shrieking gust of wind, Lulu's eyes were getting wider, and her lip was starting to quiver. They sat down on the floor. She climbed on Charlie's lap and wrapped her arms around his neck. Any second, Lulu was going to start to wail. Charlie had to think of something.

Whoooooo-eeeeeesh!

"Listen to those fairies!" Charlie exclaimed.

It was worth a try . . . and it seemed to work.

Lulu let go of his neck.

"Fairies?"

"Yes," Charlie said. "That's the sound they make when they're . . . uh . . . building a rainbow."

Mama and Papa nodded along.

"We have to stay very calm," Charlie went on. "Because if anyone cries or whines, we'll scare the fairies away before they're done."

Lulu nodded.

"Okay," she whispered.

Mama gave Charlie's leg a grateful pat.

More and more people came through the front door.

They brought stories of what was happening outside.

"I saw a huge pole flying through the sky. Like a stick."

"Four horses swam down our street."

"Houses are floating like boats."

And then the front door blew open. A woman staggered into the living room. Charlie gasped and grabbed Lulu so she wouldn't see. The woman was soaking wet and had blood dripping down her face. She stood there like a statue, her eyes wild with fear, her mouth frozen open like she was screaming. But no sound came out.

Mrs. Potts rushed over to her and quickly took her away.

The wind shrieked.

Whoooooo-eeeeeesh!

And it was at that moment when it truly hit Charlie — what this hurricane meant.

They were all safe inside this sturdy house.

But how many people were still out there? What would happen to them? When the storm was finally over, what would be left of Galveston?

The answer came in Mr. Early's voice, an echo in Charlie's mind.

"Nothing left . . . nothing at all."

CHAPTER 15

ABOUT TWO HOURS LATER
5:15 P.M.

Time crawled by. Babies were fussing. Beads of sweat dripped down Charlie's neck — it was hot and sticky in the room.

Everyone else was getting restless, too. Someone had peeked outside and reported that water was now rushing along Broadway and creeping up the Pottses' lawn.

"I don't think that's happened before," Papa said quietly.

And the wind, those shrieking gusts, were getting stronger and stronger.

Whoooooo-eeeeeesh!

Whoooooo-eeeeeesh!

Whooooooo-eeeeeesh!

"Chowie, I don't like those fairies!" Lulu cried after one terrible gust. "Make them go away!"

Charlie thought of Meraki on that stormy night at sea, doing magic tricks for the passengers as the ship was tossed by the waves. He'd brought his magic kit with him — it was in their bag upstairs. That's how he could distract Lulu — it had worked during the last storm.

Charlie went upstairs. As he headed down the hallway, he heard what sounded like a little boy crying. A kid must have wandered upstairs and gotten lost, Charlie figured. Probably he'd wanted to look at the fancy toilet, like they had.

Charlie wanted to help the poor little kid. He followed the crying to a bedroom down the hall. The door wasn't closed all the way. He peered inside.

It was not a lost little kid crying.

It was Gordon. He was sitting on his bed. Mr. Potts was standing in front of him.

"Stop your blubbering!" Mr. Potts scolded. "You know I detest crying!"

"I'm sorry, Papa! I'm just —"

"You're so weak, son," Mr. Potts said. "You need to toughen up. Come on. I want you downstairs now!"

Mr. Potts turned to leave the room. Charlie quickly ducked into the bathroom. He sat on the edge of the tub, his mind turning.

Stop your blubbering. You're so weak.

Those were the exact same words Gordon used when he picked on Charlie. How many times had Mr. Potts yelled at him like this? Did he always speak to Gordon in such a nasty way?

Gordon hadn't followed Mr. Potts downstairs; Charlie could still hear him crying.

Charlie's stomach flopped. No matter how mad Papa got at Charlie, he'd never talked to him like that.

Charlie felt sorry for Gordon. For half a second, he even wondered if should go in there, to see if Gordon was okay. But there was a big mirror in the bathroom. When Charlie stood up, he caught a glimpse of himself in the lantern light. His lip was mostly healed, but it still ached. He heard Gordon's barking laugh.

Haw! Haw! Haw!

Why should Charlie feel sorry for the bully who'd aimed a pointed stick at him?

Charlie shook his head to clear his thoughts, then headed to get his magic kit. Which trick would he do first for Lu and the other kids? The French drop? The vanishing balls?

All of them, he decided. *And I'll start with —*

Just then, panicked shouts erupted from downstairs.

"The water! It's coming into the house!"

Charlie darted to the staircase and made it halfway down before he froze. To his shock, water was rushing across the floor below. And it was rising higher by the second.

Mr. Early's voice echoed in his head.

"The sea suddenly rose up . . ."

And then a stream of panicked people came

barreling up the stairs. Charlie was caught in the stampede. The crowd pushed him forward, down the hall. Charlie didn't see Mama or Papa or Lulu anywhere.

A lantern went out, and now there was barely any light. In the rush of pushing and shoving, Charlie wound up in a dark room.

The wind let out an earsplitting shriek.

Whoo-eeeeeesh! Whoo-eeeeeesh! Whoo-eeeeeesh!

The lanterns were out in this room, too. Charlie fumbled around, pawing at the air until he hit a wall. He leaned against it, trying to brace himself as the house shook harder and harder.

Plaster rained down from the ceiling. He strained to see in the dark. Was he alone in here? Did he hear someone shouting? Or crying? Or was that just the wind?

And then came the strongest blast yet.

Whoo-eeeeeeeesh!

The wall behind him shuddered.

The sound was louder than anything Charlie had heard today.

There was another crack and the wall behind him was suddenly . . . gone.

The wind grabbed hold of Charlie and pulled him back.

"Mamaaaaa! Papaaaaa!"

Charlie was sucked out into the darkness, into the jaws of the storm.

CHAPTER 16

SPLASH.

Charlie fell hard into the cold water. The waves grabbed him, tossed him, carried him away. He sank down until his feet touched something solid. He pushed off and shot back to the surface. He came up sputtering, coughing.

He looked around but could hardly see through the pelting rain. But he knew the water was filled with wreckage. He could feel it. Every second something smacked him, scraped him, stabbed him. A barrel, a wagon wheel, part of a fence.

Charlie protected himself as best he could, but the wreckage kept coming. A dresser. A metal sign from one of the shops downtown. They slammed into him from the left and right, from in front and behind. Charlie used his arms and body to push things away. He kicked his legs hard to keep his head above the waves.

But the water was too rough.

And then, suddenly, he couldn't kick his legs. He was caught on something. With horror he wondered if it was snakes.

But no. It was rope. A piece of rope had wrapped around his legs. He kicked harder and harder, and clawed wildly at the water. But it was no use. He started to sink.

And then came a big gust of wind. Something massive smashed into Charlie's leg — a tree branch, or a light pole, maybe.

A stabbing pain shot up and down Charlie's body. He froze and couldn't move. And next thing he knew the rope had fallen away. He burst up out of the water. He managed to grab a door that was floating by, and to haul himself on top. He rolled onto his side and vomited up seawater.

He found some strength to lift his head and peer through the darkness. He couldn't see much. It was too dark. But for a few seconds, the moonlight broke through the swirl of clouds, and Charlie got a look at what was around him.

There was water, of course. But not like an overflow. Not like any flood he'd ever imagined. This was the ocean. Churning, raging ocean, for as far as he could see. It was just like Mr. Early said — Galveston swallowed up by the sea.

He saw some houses still standing, rising up out of the sea. He looked frantically for the Pottses' house. Were Mama and Papa and Lulu still safe?

The moonlight disappeared, and it was pitch-black again.

Whhhoooooossh-WOMP.

Something flew by Charlie — a brick or a roof tile, maybe — and nicked him on his chin. He cried out, then lay back down, pressing his cheek to the wet, cold wood of his door raft.

The wind shrieked.

Whoo-eeeeeesh! Whoo-eeeeeesh! Whoo-eeeeeesh!

And in between gusts, Charlie heard a shout.

"Help me! Over here!"

The waves pushed his raft closer to the shouts. It was a person, clinging to what looked like part of a wagon.

"Help me!"

Charlie managed to slow down his raft.

A sliver of moonlight lit up the person's face for a second.

It was the face that had haunted Charlie's dreams.

The wind screamed.

Whoo-eeeeeeeesh!

"Gordon?" Charlie said.

Whoo-eeeeeeeesh!

"Charlie?"

Charlie hesitated for a few seconds. This was the person who had thrown a rat at him, who had almost stabbed him with a stick.

But this was also the boy who had a papa who screamed at him. Who called him weak. Who made him cry in the middle of a hurricane.

Most of all, Gordon was a just a kid — scared and alone in the middle of this nightmare.

Like Charlie.

Charlie made room on the door, and Gordon climbed on.

They rode the waves for a few seconds, and then a huge piece of metal fence smacked Charlie in the shoulder and pushed him into the water. The waves grabbed him — but so did Gordon. He gripped Charlie's arm and pulled him back up. The door bobbed up and down, barely keeping them afloat.

They needed something bigger, stronger.

"There!" Gordon shouted. Another large shape was coming toward them — it looked like part of a roof. They clung to the door. And just as the roof sailed by, they managed to scramble onto it.

It felt more solid than the door. But the waves were already clawing it apart. It wouldn't last long.

Whoo-eeeeeeeesh! Whizzzzzz!

The wind was shooting bricks and tiles at them.

"Keep your head down!" Charlie cried out.

Whoo-eeeeeeesh! Whizzzzzz!

But even lying flat, they weren't safe. Charlie thought of Grandpa's stories of the Battle of San Jacinto, the bullets and cannonballs flying everywhere. He remembered how at one point Grandpa was trapped in a field. But he found a big fallen branch and managed to hide behind it.

He and Gordon needed something to protect their heads and backs. There was so much wreckage in the water. It didn't take long to spot a flat piece of wood.

"Gordon! Grab that."

A minute later, they'd figured out how they could lie next to each other on their stomachs, each holding an edge of the board so it covered them. Like a shield.

Charlie felt safer. But now that he didn't have to think about getting his head smashed in, other thoughts filled his mind. A new kind of terror gripped his heart.

Mama and Papa and Lulu. Were they safe? Was that house he'd seen the Pottses' house? And even if it was standing then, was it still standing now?

Boom! Boom! Boom!

And now there was thunder.

Flash!

And lightning.

Tears sprang into Charlie's eyes as he thought of Lulu.

"Please," Charlie whispered. "Please let her be safe. Let them all be safe."

He closed his eyes and imagined Lulu wrapped up in Mama's arms, with Papa hovering over them both.

Please. Please. Please, Charlie prayed. *Let them be safe. Let them be safe.*

Lightning flashed once again. Charlie opened his eyes as the flashes lit up the horrors all around.

Flash! A house on its side.

Flash! A woman clinging to a crumbling hunk of wood.

Flash! A smashed boat.

Flash! A massive wooden pole, speeding through the water.

Heading right for them.

CHAPTER 17

The pole slammed into their raft, smashing it apart. Charlie tumbled into the water. He went down, down, down — this water had to be twenty feet deep. Finally, Charlie's feet hit the ground, and he pushed off. But he only made it a few feet before something stopped him. And this time it wasn't just a piece of rope. It wasn't a snake, either.

Charlie fumbled with his fingers and felt a tangle of thin wire.

He kicked and kicked, but the wire wrapped itself tighter around his calves.

No! He reached down and tugged hard,

kicking more frantically. But now the wire was digging into his flesh.

It was hopeless.

This was it.

And it was so quiet down here. The wind wasn't shrieking. Those glass shards of rain weren't stabbing his face. No flying bricks or stones or tiles could smack him in the face.

Charlie relaxed. Maybe he should just give up. He imagined himself rising up peacefully, like that floating woman . . . up, up, up out of the water, up, up, up above those thick clouds.

He let his body go completely limp.

And then he *was* rising up. Wait! The wires had loosened! He started kicking as hard as he could again. The wires tightened. His chest was about to explode.

A thought whispered from the back of his head — something he'd heard. No, something he'd read. In Meraki's book. That new magician, Houdini.

One must not panic or struggle when trying to get free from a rope . . .

Charlie stopped kicking. His lungs felt crushed. His eyeballs felt like they were going to pop from his skull. But he somehow kept very still. He felt the wires loosening. With just the slightest wriggle of his legs, Charlie was free. Like magic.

He dropped down deeper so he could push off the bottom. With every ounce of strength he had left, he rocketed himself up, pushing away the wreckage in his path.

He broke through the surface, sucking in the air. Wind actually blew into his mouth, filling his lungs. He heard someone shouting his name.

"Charlie!"

"Gordon!"

Gordon was clinging to a new raft — a chunk of wall.

He reached out with both arms and heaved Charlie up. But this new raft was breaking up quickly, too. They had to find something strong, something that could keep them safe until all this stopped.

Flash!

Charlie saw it — a big tree that was somehow still standing.

He heard Mr. Early's voice in his mind.

"That tree — that's how I got through . . . managed to hang on until the sun came up."

"Gordon! Kick! To that tree!"

They both kicked with all their might. But the water pushed them away from the tree.

"Harder!" Charlie cried.

They kicked and kicked. Slowly they inched toward the tree.

After what seemed like hours, they were finally only a few feet away.

"On three," Charlie shouted. "One, two, three!"

They both let go of the raft and threw themselves at the tree.

Whoo-eeeeeeeesh!

The wind tried to knock them back, but they both managed to take hold of a branch. They climbed higher and nestled themselves between two thick limbs. The wind was hurling its bullets and cannonballs. But the tree seemed to wrap its strong arms around them. The water tried to snatch them back. But it couldn't reach them. He and Gordon leaned heavily against each other. Charlie held on to his branch with all his might.

The hours wore on. The wind shrieked. The rain poured down. The lightning flashed. Charlie's arms were so tired. More than once, he just wanted to let go, to slip down like a coin in a French drop, to fall into the quiet deep of the churning sea.

He was so tired and scared.

But he thought of Mama and Papa and Lulu. He told himself they were safe. That they were waiting for him, praying for him like he was praying for them.

And each time he felt himself slip from that tree, he held on tighter. He heard a voice whispering through his mind.

You are strong.

It wasn't Meraki's voice or Sarah's. It wasn't Mr. Early's or Grandpa's or even Mama's or Papa's.

At first Charlie wasn't sure whose voice it was.

And then it came to him:

It was his own.

CHAPTER 18

THE NEXT MORNING, SUNRISE
SUNDAY, SEPTEMBER 9, 1900
GALVESTON, TEXAS

Sometime after midnight, the pounding rain had slowed to a drizzle. The wind's shrieking roar had dropped to a moan, and finally a whisper. With shocking speed, the water had drained away.

When the sun started to rise, Charlie and Gordon climbed down from the tree. They stood together in the mud. Charlie stared at the shattered land around them. He turned in every direction, staring at the mountains of rubble, the heaps of wood that covered the ground as far as he could see.

Gordon gripped Charlie's hand. Neither of them spoke.

Impossible, Charlie told himself.

None of this was real.

Not the wrecked houses lying like smashed eggs. Not the people, dazed, bloodied, weeping.

No. This wasn't real. Charlie saw it. But he wouldn't believe it. Because what he was seeing was impossible.

He and Gordon started to walk. Each time Charlie saw something new, that word screamed through his mind.

The woman sobbing as she clawed through what was left of a house.

Impossible.

The pile of stones where a church had once stood.

Impossible.

A mountain of wreckage in the distance, taller than any building, stretching for blocks and blocks to the gulf.

Impossible.

The hand poking out from under a pile of wood.

Impossible.

This was all a trick. An evil, terrible trick. A trick on his eyes. His ears. His heart.

He thought only of his family. It was their faces he kept in his mind as he and Gordon tried to make their way back to Broadway. It took a very long time.

But finally, there was Gordon's house — still standing, though sagging, with parts of the roof and walls missing.

Mr. Potts was on the steps. He let out a sob of joy when he saw Gordon.

"Son!"

Gordon staggered forward, and his father grabbed him and lifted him off the ground. Mrs. Pott appeared and rushed to join them.

But Charlie just stood there. Where were Mama and Papa and Lulu?

Charlie dropped his eyes. His mind started to spin.

And then . . .

"*Chowie!*"

Charlie looked up. Papa was running toward him. Mama was right behind him, carrying Lulu. Charlie fell to his knees. It seemed he'd been floating through the air, twisting and turning in those dark clouds. But now somehow he'd made it back onto the ground.

Arms came around him.

They were all safe.

It was impossible.

It was true.

CHAPTER 19

ABOUT SIX MONTHS LATER
MARCH 16, 1901
AROUND 7:00 P.M.
CHARLIE'S SCHOOL
GALVESTON, TEXAS

Loud noises rose up all around Charlie.

Balls bouncing. A piano playing. Kids laughing. Sarah's voice.

"Charlie!"

Charlie turned from the window. Sarah grinned at him as she tightened the laces of her tap shoes.

"Don't you think you should get ready? You're going onstage first!"

It was the night of the school talent show, and they were backstage, in the school auditorium. Their teacher, Mrs. Butler, was helping one of the girls fasten a ribbon into her hair.

"It's crowded out there," said Charlie's new friend Lee, bouncing one of the balls he'd be juggling in his act.

Rosemary Cline walked over to Charlie. She was singing a song in the show. "Charlie," she said, smiling. "Your mustache is crooked."

She was talking about the fake mustache Mama had made for him, out of some scraps of fabric — he had wanted a mustache like Meraki's. Charlie thanked Rosemary and went to the mirror next to the window.

He realized now that his mustache actually looked like a very sick caterpillar. And it itched. Charlie peeled it off and tossed it in the trash.

He peered into the mirror again, relieved to see his familiar freckled face. He was still getting used to the big scar on his chin — from a flying roof tile. The scar turned bright red when he got cold, but it didn't hurt anymore.

He had bigger scars. His body was covered with jagged lines, puckers, and dents, all from his time in the churning water. Charlie closed his eyes and tried to stop the swirl of memories. But he suddenly felt like he was floating, like he was in the air, spinning, twisting, unable to get himself back onto solid ground. It happened all the time lately. At school. At the dinner table. On the street. He'd suddenly feel far away, back in those terrible hours and days after the storm.

And now his mind swirled with the nightmare memories — the sobs of neighbors, the sight of their shattered house. Standing in line in the roasting heat, waiting for bread and drinkable water. Sleeping on the floor of the church. The terrible smells that rose from the wreckage.

Charlie tried to remember how lucky he was. Unlike thousands of other people, he'd made it out of the water that night.

Nobody knew exactly how many thousands had died. Six thousand? Eight thousand? And that was just on Galveston Island. It was impossible to know because so many had been swept out to sea. Entire families were gone.

And Galveston — more than half the city had been completely destroyed. Houses and buildings. Churches. Schools. Stores. Blocks and blocks along the beach had been scraped clean by the raging sea, everything smashed up and pushed into a giant mountain. That's what he and Gordon had seen when they had climbed down from the tree.

After ten days, Mama and Charlie and Lulu left the city along with most of Galveston's women and children. They took a crowded barge across the bay. Mama took them to Houston to stay with her cousins.

Papa stayed behind — they needed men to clear away wreckage.

When Mama brought Charlie and Lulu back to the city, three months later, almost all the rubble was gone. Charlie was shocked to see trains chugging across the bay again. Wagons and buggies and carriages crowded the streets. The sounds of hammers and saws drifted through the air. The streetcar dinged.

School opened right before Christmas.

A firm hand took hold of his shoulder. He felt a jolt, like he was waking up from a dream. And there was Sarah, right in front of him, watching him with her gleaming eyes. "You all right?" she asked.

Charlie had never told her about the floating. But somehow she always knew how to bring him back. She kept her hand on his shoulder, gripping it tightly, as though she was holding him down to the ground.

It took a moment for Charlie's mind to stop swirling. He looked out the window again.

The sky was bright, with just a few puffy clouds. In the distance was the Gulf, silvery blue, calm as a pond.

Charlie nodded to Sarah.

Mrs. Butler rushed over. "Ready for you, Charlie!"

Charlie patted his pockets, making sure he had his cards and coins.

Lee and Rosemary wished him luck. Other kids smiled and waved.

"Go, Charlie!"

"You'll be great!"

Charlie walked slowly onto the stage. The auditorium erupted into cheers and applause.

"Chowie!" a voice shrieked.

There was Lulu on Mama's lap, waving like a maniac from the front row. Mama beamed up at him. Papa's eyes sparkled with pride.

Behind them were Mr. and Mrs. Potts. They both waved — Mr. Potts was almost smiling. And Gordon . . . he grinned and waved, too.

They were friends now — how could they not be after what they'd been through? Gordon had apologized about the rat and the pointed branch, over and over. Charlie forgave him — and told him his whole cockroach plan. Gordon laughed his head off.

The applause died down.

Charlie just stood there, staring out at the audience, at all these people. Somehow they'd made it through the storm.

Impossible.

But so many were missing — parents, grandparents, kids he'd known his whole life. Mr. Early hadn't made it, either. They were all gone forever.

Impossible.

Charlie got that floating feeling again. But his eyes caught Lulu's. And then Mama's and Papa's.

He clenched his fists and lifted his chin. He stepped forward, into a circle of glittering light, and took a breath.

"Ladies and gentlemen," he shouted, in his loudest, clearest voice. "I am Charles the Great!"

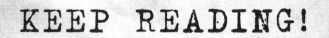

KEEP READING!

Turn the page to find out why
Lauren Tarshis wrote about the
Galveston hurricane and to learn more
facts about hurricanes and life in 1900.

People swimming near the Pagoda Bathhouse, in 1895.

Galveston's beach today. The Pagoda was never rebuilt. But the Pleasure Pier attracts fun seekers from around the U.S.

WRITING ABOUT THE GALVESTON HURRICANE

Dear Readers,

Kids often ask me how I decide what events to write about in the I Survived series. It's a great question, because I have written about many kinds of events — natural disasters and wars, accidents and attacks. Some are famous — like the American Revolution. Others are little known, like the Great Boston Molasses Flood.

I find ideas everywhere — books I read, places I travel to, museums I explore, and, best of all, readers like you. There are so many fascinating and important topics.

So how do I choose?

I look for events that changed our world or our ideas. The American Revolution, of course, led to the United States becoming its own country. The Boston Molasses Flood led to laws that make the buildings we live in today safer.

Market Street in Galveston's downtown, in 1894. Look closely and you'll see the streetcar coming toward you. What else do you notice?

So what about the Galveston hurricane?

Of course the storm changed the lives of everyone who was in Galveston on that terrible day. Thousands died. Thousands more were injured and lost their homes.

The storm also changed the history of Texas. Until September 8, 1900, Galveston was the fastest-growing city in the American South. Galveston was locked in a competition with Houston to become the third-largest city in Texas, and Galveston was about to take the lead.

Following the storm, Galveston was rebuilt with shocking speed. But it never regained its former place as a powerful Texas city. Today, Houston is the biggest city in Texas by far (about 2,300,000 people lived there). San Antonio is second, Dallas a close third, followed by Austin, the Texas capital.

And Galveston? Today it is ranked sixty-eighth in population in the state. Just 50,400 people live there, fewer than in many medium-sized towns.

Perhaps most important: The Galveston hurricane showed what happens when we try to ignore the power of nature. Most people in Galveston really did believe that it was impossible for a powerful hurricane to strike their city.

They believed this even though their city sits on a flat island surrounded by the sea.

They believed this even though the city was constantly being flooded.

And they believed this even though Galveston had been destroyed before.

So why did so many sensible people believe that Galveston couldn't be struck

This question echoed through my mind as I researched this book. I couldn't find a simple answer. It's true that scientists were just beginning to understand the science of weather in 1900. There wasn't much information. And if you wanted to learn about hurricanes, you couldn't just google it. Remember, this storm happened 1900. Google? iPhones? Such technology was a century away. You would have been lucky to find a single weather book in a library.

Even so, people didn't need Google to realize that Galveston faced a huge hurricane risk. It was obvious. So — again — why did so many people ignore the risks? I think the main reason is the simplest: It was easier. Thinking about a powerful hurricane is scary. And remember Galveston's race with Houston. Galveston's

In 1899, Galveston was the fastest growing city in the South — and one of the richest in the world. Notice all the different kinds of buggies and carriages. At the time, the first motorcars were appearing on American streets.

leaders wanted their city to keep growing. But would people want to move to a city that lay in the path of dangerous hurricanes? Maybe not.

But the hurricane in Galveston taught people how dangerous it is to deny the risk of a powerful storm. To be fair, in 1900, people had fewer tools for predicting when and where hurricanes could strike. But there were still steps Galveston's leaders could have taken to educate people about storms, to better protect the city's residents.

Today we have far more ways to keep ourselves safe. Satellites in space keep an eye on Earth;

weather scientists spot hurricanes almost the moment they form over our oceans. Computers help weather experts plot where a storm might strike. People living in a storm's path get lots of warning so they can prepare — or escape— before it's too late.

Writing this book was painful at times. I kept thinking about how the people of Galveston suffered. My heart kept breaking as I read stories of real people who suffered through that day.

And there was something else going on while I was writing this book — the COVID-19 pandemic. It was a dark and difficult time for all of us.

To all of you readers, parents, and teachers, I want you to know how much you brightened my days. I met hundreds of you during virtual visits. I loved your questions and your smiles. You teachers inspired me with your dedication.

I feel lucky, as always, to be a part of your world.

With admiration and gratitude,

THE GALVESTON HURRICANE BY THE NUMBERS

- Between **6,000** and **12,000** people died
- More than **7,000** buildings were destroyed, including **3,600** houses
- **10,000** people were left homeless
- The mountain of debris after the storm was **3** miles long and **30** feet high
- **25** churches were destroyed

MORE FACTS

THE GALVESTON HURRICANE IS STILL THE DEADLIEST NATURAL DISASTER IN AMERICAN HISTORY

After the storm, the official death toll was set at 6,000. However, experts agree it was far higher. The exact figure can't be known because so many people were swept out to sea.

No other U.S. natural disaster has come close to taking as many lives. The San Francisco earthquake and fire, which happened six years later, in 1906, killed about 3,000.

HURRICANES ARE THE MOST VIOLENT STORMS ON EARTH

The more I learn about hurricanes, the more I think that Lulu had the right idea when she imagined the cloud monster. These storms really are monstrous!

No storms are bigger. No storms pack more destructive power. But what exactly are hurricanes?

They are big, swirling storms with winds that are at least 74 miles per hour. These storms create enormous amounts of rain. They gain strength over oceans, feeding on the warm, moist air over the water. They range in size from 100 miles to more than 1,000 miles wide.

A hurricane packs three dangerous forces:

- Winds, which can rip apart houses and topple trees
- Rain, in enormous quantities, which can cause flooding
- The "storm surge," a wall of ocean water that is pushed onto land by the hurricane's winds.

It is estimated that the storm surge sent 15 feet of water rushing over Galveston.

Today, hurricanes are given a rank based on the strength of their winds. A category 1 storm is the weakest. Category 5 are the true monsters, with winds that can reach 200 miles per hour. These rankings didn't exist in 1900, but experts say the Galveston hurricane would have been a category 4.

Weather satellites in the sky take pictures that show us hurricanes as they move across the oceans. Notice the swirling shape, and the tiny hole in the center. That hole is called the "eye." The strongest hurricane winds are right next to the eye.

THE GALVESTON HURRICANE WAS BORN IN AFRICA, 5,000 MILES AWAY

So are most of the powerful hurricanes that strike land along the America's eastern and southern coasts. These monstrous storms begin over the Sahara desert. Hot desert air meets moist air from the Indian Ocean. High in the sky, bundles of clouds gather together. These are known as "easterly waves."

Every few days, an "easterly" leaves the African coast and heads west over the Atlantic Ocean. Most of them die out quickly. But some keep chugging along until they reach a group of islands off the African coast. These are the Cape Verde islands. And this is where trouble often begins. It's here that these easterly clouds can grow and transform into thunderstorms. Winds start to swirl, sucking in energy from the moist air over the ocean.

They start to move east again, gaining speed and power from the moist ocean air — and at some point, they become hurricanes.

Not all hurricanes that hit the U.S. are these "Cape Verde" hurricanes. Other powerful hurricanes can form in Caribbean Sea or in the Gulf of Mexico. But over the past 200 years, 85 percent of the biggest and most powerful hurricanes to hit the United States have been Cape Verde hurricanes.

The Cape Verde islands off the coast of Africa.

DR. ISAAC CLINE WAS A REAL PERSON

He was the head of the Galveston Weather Bureau, and a respected weather expert. He was married and had three daughters — Rosemary was his middle daughter. Dr. Cline really did believe that Galveston could not be hit by a powerful hurricane. In 1891, he wrote an article in the *Galveston Daily News*. In it, he wrote that it would be "impossible" for a hurricane to "create a storm wave that would . . . injure the city."

Early Friday morning, the day before the storm, Dr. Cline noticed that the Gulf was behaving strangely. It looked very calm. But every few minutes, the water would seem to rise up by a few feet and then go down again. Dr. Cline knew these rises were caused by "deep water swells." These were a sign that not so far away, a big storm was churning up the Gulf.

Dr. Cline grew more and more nervous throughout Friday, and by Saturday morning,

he was convinced that a hurricane was coming. In the end, his own house was washed away. He and his three daughters survived. His wife, Cora, did not.

Dr. Isaac Cline was a widely respected scientist in Galveston and within the U.S. Weather Bureau.

GALVESTON IS NOW PROTECTED BY A GIANT SEAWALL

In 1886, town leaders discussed building a seawall to protect Galveston. This came after a hurricane destroyed the nearby city of Indianola, about 150 miles to the southwest. But Galveston's leaders rejected the idea of building a wall. It would cost millions — and take years. And why bother since (they believed) a similar hurricane could not strike their city?

And then came the 1900 hurricane.

In 1902, construction began on a 17-foot-tall, 3-mile-wide-long wall of concrete, wood, stone, and steel. It was completed in 1904 and was later lengthened. Today it is ten miles long.

The Galveston seawall, completed in 1904, helps protect the city from punishing hurricane waves.

Even more remarkable, 500 blocks of Galveston were raised up during one of the most amazing engineering projects of the early twentieth century. Between 1903 and 1911, more than 3,000 buildings — houses, churches, businesses — were raised up onto jacks or stilts.

Sand and mud was dug up or "dredged" from near Galveston Bay. This sandy muck was piped underneath the buildings, which were then lowered back onto the ground. During these years, people walked along raised walkways that zigzagged the city.

What a mess!

But when this project was finished, much of Galveston was between 8 and 17 feet higher, and better protected from floods and storms.

During years that Galveston was being raised up, it was known as the "City on Stilts."

ANOTHER MAJOR HURRICANE STRUCK GALVESTON IN 1915

The winds did not reach the same strength as the 1900 storm. But the hurricane hovered over the coast for twice as long, hammering the city with powerful winds, drenching it with record-breaking amounts of rain. The entire downtown was flooded with at least 6 feet of water. But the seawall did its job. Waves pounded against it for hours and hours, but the wall stood firm. Houses were destroyed, but only those that were behind the reach of the wall.

Only 11 people in the city lost their lives.

Still, the storm caused millions of dollars of damage. Every ship in the port was destroyed. The cleanup took months. This storm, coming only 15 years after the first, was another reminder of Galveston's hurricane risk.

IN 1900, MAGICIANS WERE HUGE CELEBRITIES

You've probably heard of Harry Houdini. In 1900, he was just one of several world-famous magicians dazzling the world with their shows. Back then, kids didn't play video games or watch streaming shows. Magic was a wildly popular hobby — every kid wanted their own magic kit. This was the "golden age" of magic.

Professional magicians were the most famous performers in the world. Houdini was just getting started in 1900. Far more famous was a man named Harry Kellar. Imagine your favorite athlete, singer, TV star, and YouTuber all combined into one superstar. That was Harry Kellar. He was even the inspiration for the wizard in *The Wizard of Oz*.

I've tried a few times to slip Harry Kellar into my I Survived books. And I was determined to put him front and center in this book. I read all about him and became fascinated by his tricks. Especially that ring trick, when he crushed the ring, sprinkled the powder into a gun, and

Harry Kellar and Harry Houdini

An advertisement for one of Harry Kellar's magic shows.

made it appear in a box. (It was actually more complicated when he performed it. After many drafts, I decided to make it simpler for Charlie's story.)

How did he do it? None of the books revealed this secret.

So I got in touch with one of today's famous magicians, Dean Carnegie. He said that kind of trick was pretty common in those days. He explained that Kellar didn't really crush the ring. He'd slipped them into his pocket and pretended to crush them. The box was a trick box, with some kind of opening in the box that let him slip the ringinside before he opened it.

Amazing!

But in the end, Kellar didn't make it into my book. I decided to make up my own magician, Antonio Meraki. I included some details I learned from Kellar — like the ring trick. But I had the freedom to create fictional details so they worked better with Charlie and his journey.

I chose the name Meraki because it's one of my favorite words. It's Greek, and it means a special kind of joy you feel when you put your heart and soul into something you love to do.

And that's how I feel when I'm writing these books for you — *meraki*.

HOW TO STAY SAFE IN A HURRICANE

Storms are frightening to think about. It's so much easier to put them out of our minds. But that's not a good idea. Being prepared can actually make us feel less scared — and safer if a storm actually hits.

Here's how you and your family can get started.

1. KNOW YOUR RISK

Do you live near an ocean, a gulf, a sea or a sound? (I do.) Then you could experience a hurricane. And even if you don't live right on the water, there are still big risks from the winds and the rains.

It's also helpful to learn about hurricanes that happened in the past.

2. HELP YOUR FAMILY MAKE A PLAN

Luckily, today we get plenty of warnings before storms. If necessary, you and your family might decide to leave your home — evacuate — until the storm is over and it's safe to return. It's a good idea for you and your family to talk about this. Where would you go? What would you take with you?

You can also talk to your teacher at school about inviting someone from your town's police or fire department to come talk to your class about being prepared.

3. DON'T GO OUTSIDE DURING A HURRICANE

People can get badly hurt by trees and other objects picked up by the wind (remember Charlie and those cannonball bricks). Never go to the beach to look at the stormy sea. Even after a storm is over, be careful. Never go near a wire that has been brought down by the wind — you could get shocked. Even after the storm is over, be careful of trees that could be damaged and may have cracked limbs.

4. HELP THOSE IN NEED

Every year, millions of people around the world are impacted by extreme weather like hurricanes. You and your friends can help them by raising money and donating clothing and other supplies. Have your parents or teacher help you. Always work with an experienced and trusted aid organization that will make sure your donation goes to people in need.

Some suggestions:
Save the Children
savethechildren.org
American Red Cross
redcross.org
World Vision
worldvision.org

Lauren Tarshis's *New York Times* bestselling I Survived series tells stories of young people and their resilience and strength in the midst of unimaginable disasters and times of turmoil. Lauren has brought her signature warmth, integrity, and exhaustive research to topics such as the September 11 attacks, the American Revolution, Hurricane Katrina, the bombing of Pearl Harbor, and other world events. Lauren lives in Connecticut with her family, and can be found online at laurentarshis.com.